Baby Days

CAROL
THOMPSON

ORCHARD BOOKS

to Rosemary

Text and illustrations copyright © Carol Thompson 1991
First published in Great Britain in 1991 by
ORCHARD BOOKS
96 Leonard Street, London EC2A 4RH
Orchard Books Australia
14 Mars Road, Lane Cove NSW 2066
1 85213 288 4
A CIP catalogue record for this book
is available from the British Library.
Printed in Hong Kong

CONTENTS

1
GETTING UP

A Dressing Rhyme

I can tie my shoelaces,	*I can brush my hair,*	*I can wash my hands and face*	*And dry myself with care.*

I can clean my teeth, too,	*And fasten up my frocks,*	*I can dress all by myself*	*And pull up both my socks.*

It's fun to put on clothes

. . . or wear no clothes at all.

These are clothes that babies wear.

2
BABIES CAN DO
LOTS OF THINGS

Babies can . . .

stand

sit

bend down

look up

look down

turn around

pull

crawl

lie down

walk

run

jump

crouch

push

11

Action Rhymes

Heads and shoulders, knees and toes,

And eyes and ears and mouth and nose.

Can you walk on tiptoe
As softly as a cat?

And can you stamp along the road
Stamp, stamp, just like that?

Can you take some great big strides
Just like a giant can?

Or walk along so slowly
Like a bent old man?

3
PLAYING

Babies can play with anything.

They like playing with their toys.

They play inside and outside.

la la la

toot toot

boom boom

jingle jangle

crash bang

They like playing noisy games . . .

and quiet games.

A Playing Rhyme

Two little eyes to look around,
Two little ears to hear each sound;
One little nose to smell what's sweet,
One little mouth that likes to eat.

4
MEALTIMES

Babies enjoy their food.

They drink milk from their mothers

and from bottles and cups.

Babies like eating . . .

potatoes

biscuits

bananas

fish fingers

bread

grapes

apples

pears

peas

eggs

carrots

rice

celery

cereal

cheese

tangerines

5
GOING OUT

Babies like going anywhere.

They like going to the playground

or to the supermarket.

Babies go out in . . .

buggies

carrycots

baby slings

baby carriers

and on Dad's bike.

Babies like going out on hot days

and on cold days,

on wet days

and on windy days.

6
ANIMALS

Animals love babies.

And babies
love animals.

prrrr

purrr

mmooooo

An Animal Rhyme

I love little pussy,
Her coat is so warm,
And if I don't hurt her
She'll do me no harm.

So I'll not pull her tail
Nor drive her away,

But pussy and I
Very gently will play.

7
FEELINGS

Babies feel . . .

quiet

helpful

sleepy

cross

brave

wet

warm

happy

Sometimes babies don't feel well

. . . but they soon feel better.

8
GOING TO BED

Babies have a bath
before they go to bed.

They like splashing in the water

and getting dry again.

45

Babies like a story at bedtime

... and soon they're fast asleep.

Bedtime Rhymes

Golden slumbers kiss your eyes;
Smiles awake you when you rise.
Sleep, pretty baby, do not cry,
And I will sing you a lullaby.

Star light, star bright,
First star I see tonight.
I wish I may, I wish I might,
Have the wish I wish tonight.